Praise for *Skin Over Milk*

Skin Over Milk tells the story of young Chutki and her two sisters who bear the weight of being unwanted daughters in 1990's India. Told through Chutki's eyes, we feel the innocence that is childhood, allowing the gratitude for a crust of bread thrown away by her brothers, or the simple joy in making prank phone calls. We meet characters, such as the father who curses their mother for giving him useless girls, the brothers who don't seem to appreciate the luxury of education. But we also meet the loving grandfather, Dada, who will die and watch over them like a star in the sky and their beautiful, beautiful mother, Ammi, who does what she can to make all of their lives bearable. Exquisitely written with a jeweler's eye for detail, the deftest of hands with characterization and storytelling, this is a brilliant and unforgettable read.

— Francine Witte, author of *Dressed All Wrong for This* and *The Way of the Wind*

"The summer of 1990 brought rain and more rain to our little town of Muzaffarnagar." Thus begins Sara Chansarkar's chapbook, *Skin Over Milk*, an elegantly written and immersive family story told over the course of twelve short chapters and through the collective point of view of the family's siblings. We readers get a strong sense of this particular family's joys and heartaches, struggles and traditions. Chansarkar knows how to weave her stories seamlessly and disarmingly, with heart and humor and tenderness. It is a testament to this writer's mastery that I never wanted the story to end.

— Kathy Fish, author of *Wild Life: Collected Works*

With precision and insight, these evocative stories within a story speak of rain and tears, of sisterhood and solidarity, of poverty, and growing up as girls under the lashes of patriarchy. Chansarkar evokes the poetry and brutality of small-town India with a deftness that makes it impossible to tell which is which.

— Damyanti Biswas, author of *You Beneath Your Skin* and *The Blue Bar*

In lush and incisive prose, Sara Siddiqui Chansarkar tells the story of three sisters growing up in a home and a culture that treats them as valueless, who nonetheless scheme and dream to claim space: "I sat squished between my sisters, dreaming of a seat of my own someday." Like the secret a mother whispers in the ear of her crying baby girl to protect her from her husband's rage, *Skin Over Milk* is confiding, talismanic. By turns painful and joyful, this novella transfixed me.

— Kim Magowan, author of *Undoing, The Light Source*, and *How Far I've Come*

Skin Over Milk

Chestnut Review
Ithaca, New York
https://chestnutreview.com
ISBN: 9798834961567

Skin Over Milk

Sara Siddiqui Chansarkar

Chestnut Review Chapbooks

For my Ammi and my sisters

CONTENTS

Skin Over Milk

The summer of 1990 brought rain and more rain to our little town of Muzaffarnagar. We sisters—eleven, ten, and nine at the time—heard it through the quiet of the night, drumming on the mango leaves, beating over the asbestos-awning, pouring down the tin gutters, not knowing we'd remember that rain for the rest of our lives, or that I, the youngest, would write about it one day.

By morning, murky water from the flooded drain across the alley had seeped into our cemented courtyard, slithered under the door sills of the three bedrooms—ours, our brothers', and our parents'—lined along to the right of the open space. To the left stood an old mango tree, its roots erupting from the floor in places. Across the courtyard sat the kitchen skirted with a corrugated awning, our grandfather Dada's room, the bathroom, and the bicycle shed with a tin roof.

Our nostrils caught the stench of rotting trash and urine from the drain water mingled with the fragrance of jasmine flowers that our mother Ammi grew in clay pots lined along the perimeter of the courtyard. We liked to string the flowers, sometimes, and pin them to our mother's straight, black hair.

Ammi called us, "Badki, Manjhli, Chutki, come." She said our names in the same order—from oldest to youngest. In fact, our names translated to just that: older one, middle one, younger one. Not a deeper meaning or significance to them. We assembled in the order of our heights like the steps of a stairwell—Badki, the tallest, as tall as Ammi, Manjhli shorter by an inch, and I, shorter by two inches.

On Ammi's cue, we knotted our black hair into buns, rolled up our salwar cuffs, and followed our short, slim-hipped mother, as she marched on with quick steps, silver anklets tinkling on her feet, her linen dupatta tied around her narrow waist. Our Ammi was light-skinned, her skin the golden of wheat, but we had inherited some of the dark coloring from our father, Abba. We were brown like the surface of the areca nuts we chopped into pieces for Ammi's betel-leaf treat—the paan—that she chewed at the end of each long, exhausting day.

Using a broom made of palm sticks held together with twine, Ammi raked out broken bowls, putrefying peels, and spent slippers from the drain, which gurgled with relief as water started trickling down. We grabbed wipers—rubber blades attached to long aluminum rods—and pushed the water out of the courtyard into the brick-lined alley.

Dada used to help with the rainwater but the last two times when he did that, the chill seeped into his bones, bringing along a fevered cold and a hacking cough that lingered for days. His aging body wasn't as strong as it had been before.

When we came back inside to our room after draining away the water and drying our feet with towels, Abba was still spurt-snoring in our parents' bedroom. We heard our brothers, Asif and Salman, wake up with loud, lazy yawns in their room. They were slightly older than us—aged thirteen and twelve—and much taller. Their skin was a different brown, the color of the first potatoes of the season. Asif, the eldest, had recently sprouted a thin line of hair on his upper lip. His voice had changed into a hoarse croak that sounded funny to us. Both of the boys bathed and dressed for school in shirts we'd ironed, ties we'd knotted, and shoes we'd polished the night before.

Following our morning routine, Badki walked our brothers' bicycles out of the tin shed into the courtyard, Manjhli dusted the seats with a rag, and I inflated the tires with a pump. Then I raised the rear wheel of one bicycle and pushed the pedals with my arms. We watched the spokes spin into a blur, and imagined riding the bicycles to places, real and imaginary, the breeze kissing our cheeks, but we knew we would never get to experience that because Abba kept the bicycle shed locked. Once, when our brothers returned from school, I asked Salman to teach us how to ride the two-wheeler but he scoffed at the idea.

Dressed in their school uniform of white shirts, gray ties, and navy blue trousers, Asif and Salman sat on low stools with woven seats in the kitchen for their breakfast that began with a handful of almonds. Abba said the nuts were a ghiza—nutrition—for those who studied math and science at school, so Ammi soaked them in water overnight to soften them for her sons, the heritors of our parents' adoration.

We imagined the nuts crumbling between our incisors, pulverizing between our molars, coating our tongues with pasty sweetness, but under Ammi's hawk-like vigilance and the locked food cabinet, we would never get to relish the taste.

After the almonds, Ammi served paranthas—dough discs that she rolled out with great care and pan-fried in spoonfuls of aromatic ghee—in steel plates. Then, she poured steaming milk into tall tumblers for our brothers. The stream of milk in the air between the pot and the tumblers made our stomachs thunder and our mouths rain.

We waited for Asif and Salman to finish their meal. When they were ready, Badki helped button their raincoats over their uniforms, Manjhli wrapped their book bags in cellophane sheets, and I tied grocery bags around their shoes so they wouldn't get soaked in the rain. After they left, we joined their two low stools to seat the three of us, barely, for breakfast. I sat squished between my sisters, dreaming of a seat of my own someday.

Ammi heated up stale rotis for us and smeared them with pungent mustard oil as the aroma of ghee lingered in our noses. Then, she poured chai made with little milk into our cups with broken handles. We cracked the hard roti between our teeth, moistened the morsels with our saliva but left untouched the chai—brown like the muddy drain water. I peeked inside Asif's tumbler, still a quarter full after he left in a hurry and watched a skin form over the milk.

Under the Rickshaw Hood

One morning, after the incessant pounding of rain tempered down to a rhythmic pitter-patter, we heard the rat-a-tat-tat of the metal knocker on the front door which was patched with aluminum scraps in places where the wood had rotted. We ran across the courtyard to answer the unexpected knock, our rubber slippers slapping the floor.

A scrawny, mud-skinned rickshawallah stood by his cycle rickshaw, a gray plastic sheet tied around his neck, flowing down his back. He looked like the flying man in the thin books Asif and Salman read and exchanged with their friends. Superman comics, they called them. A grocery bag covered the man's hair, which would have been silver-black, given the medley of color we observed in his facial hair. He said Abba had hired him to take our brothers to school on rainy mornings. We held our dupattas to our noses against the tobacco breath escaping his crooked beedi-stained teeth.

He inserted brickbats under the rickshaw's rear wheels to keep it from rolling away—though our house wasn't on a slope—and limped towards the amla tree by the drain, a few feet from our door. Though he stood hidden behind the thick tree trunk, we could see the arc of his yellow urine hitting the drain water. We didn't understand why men couldn't sit and urinate like we did, why they made such a spectacle of their body waste.

Sometimes, when Ammi left the house to buy vegetables from the corner shop, our brothers stood in the courtyard with their backs to us and challenged each other over the arcs their urine could draw, betting whose stream could reach the front door. The urine dried before Ammi returned but the stench lingered, and she scolded us for not shooing the street dogs away from the house, for letting them urinate at our doorstep. Something we knew that she didn't—the difference between dog and human smells.

The rickshawallah had raised the collapsible rexine hood hinged at the sides of the rickshaw to cover the passenger seat like an umbrella. The blue plastic cover of the seat was ripped, coconut-coir filling peeked out from spots across its surface. We climbed on the seat and huddled under the coziness of the hood, keeping a watch for the rickshawallah. A circle of smoke rose from behind the tree, followed by a succession of noises—throat-clearing, hacking out phlegm, and spitting. Clearly, the man was smoking a beedi.

Emboldened by his extended break, we whispered to each other and decided to take turns on the driver seat. Being the youngest, I hopped on first, but my feet couldn't reach the pedals. I moved my legs drawing circles in the air, propelling us through a pretend-tour of the town. My sisters pretend-ordered me to take them to the soda-lemonade shop which popped up by the market in summer and was nothing more than a tarp tied between bamboo poles.

Every year, the day their final exams ended, Abba took our brothers to the market and treated them to soda-lemonade. A reward for work that had yet to show results. We had gone to the lemonade shop, last summer, with Naani, Ammi's mother, when she visited.

We licked our lips, remembering the fizz and tartness of the soda-lemonade.

"Which route should I take to the market?" I asked my sisters.

"Through College Road, of course," Badki replied.

"Yes, I want to see boys and girls, walking together," Manjhli said, and added after a breath, "talking together, happily, with jute book bags slung on their shoulders."

On her turn, Manjhli's feet couldn't touch the rubber of the pedals either, but Badki's legs were longer. She pushed her feet with all her strength and managed to budge the rickshaw from its standing position. Manjhli and I pursed our lips to contain our excitement and brought our palms together for soundless claps, fearing the rickshawallah might hear us. But, Badki, taking her role as the driver to a new level, pressed her thumb over the metal bell fitted on the handlebar to indicate to the pretend-pedestrians that our vehicle was approaching. On hearing the trill, the rickshawallah limped out from behind the tree, brandishing the red tip of his beedi, yelling at us to keep away from his vehicle, the source of his livelihood.

We jumped off the rickshaw, made hand-horns in the air, and stuck our tongues out to tease the man. He screamed slurs at us: awara, kambakht, besharm. Stray, ill-fated, shameless. I called him a lame pisser. He picked a rock from the ground and threatened to hurl it at us as if we were street dogs, deserving to be shooed away. We ran inside and shut the door. He pounded at the door hard, the rusted knocker bearing the brunt of his anger. We growled and howled in response.

Piercings

Because it rained most evenings, we couldn't play hopscotch or hide-and-seek or jump rope in the courtyard. Clever Badki suggested another pastime: eavesdropping on our parents' conversation when Abba ate dinner while Ammi waved a punkah—a hand-held fan woven from bamboo strips—to circulate the air around his face.

We discussed, and identified our grandfather Dada's room, as the ideal spot for spying. Dada and his rose-ringed parakeet Mithu lived in the room across the courtyard, beside the kitchen.

Once, we'd heard Ammi talking to our Naani about how Abba's mother, dead before I was born, had poisoned her son's mind against girl children. Deeming Ammi's womb cursed, Abba's mother had advised her son to marry another woman who could give him more sons. Naani said it was sad how women were an enemy of their own kind, and it was good that Abba's mother died before forcing her son into another marriage.

Dada was matchstick-thin, cottonwool-bearded, and bamboo-tall—the tallest man we'd known, and the kindest. He didn't raise his voice at us, didn't deny our requests that were within his power and means to fulfill. There was nothing in common between him and our burly, angry Abba. He said he'd always wanted a daughter but never had one.

At night, when Ammi called Abba for his meal, we took our positions in Dada's room, atop the plateau of blankets and quilts stacked against the wall common with the kitchen for everyone to use in winter. We knew we could trust Dada—the keeper of our secrets and warm covers.

Through the wall, we heard Ammi say, "Dada has volunteered to pierce the girls' ears."

When talking about us, our parents referred to us as "girls." Always a collective.

"Why?" Abba said, annoyed. "I don't have money to buy silver or gold for your girls' ears. There's not a paisa left in my pocket after paying for Asif's and Salman's school fees."

"Don't you worry," Ammi replied, her glass bangles tinkling with the action of waving the fan. "I have some money saved from sewing the neighbors' clothes. I'll work more. We can't get the girls married off without getting their ears pierced. Better do it now before the lobes become too hard."

"Okay, whatever," Abba said in an exasperated voice. "Just don't bother me. A man can't even have a meal in peace in this house." With that, he rose and pushed the stool to the wall behind which we were crouched. We shuddered as his anger permeated through the brick and cement to us.

The next day, after Abba left for work and our brothers for school, we pressed Dada's feet, massaged his scalp, and cajoled him into piercing our ears. We couldn't wait to wear thin gold earrings like Ammi, though she had only that one pair, gifted on her wedding by Naani.

Dada asked Ammi's permission to pierce our ears. She nodded while spooling thread on the bobbin of her sewing machine. Then, he asked us to collect the things needed for the ceremony, as he called it, and himself went out to buy something important.

We followed his instructions: Badki asked Ammi for her thinnest needle and a spool of black thread, Manjhli fetched a candle and a matchbox, I got green peppers from the kitchen though I couldn't comprehend why Dada needed those for the piercing.

Dada returned with a paper bag clutched in his hands. He examined and approved the items we arranged on the rickety table beside his narrow bed. He pulled out a lump of beeswax from his sundry box, which he rubbed on the black thread, saying it would make the thread stronger than silver. We believed our grandfather, our fountain of knowledge.

Then, Dada adjusted his glasses on his nose, threaded the needle with the waxed thread, and motioned for Badki to sit on the plastic stool facing his chair. He pulled up her hair in a high ponytail and gave her a piece of lemon candy from the paper bag. Manjhli and I eyed the opaque bag, awaiting our turn to roll the lump of sugar in our mouths.

With a ballpoint pen, Dada dotted Badki's lobes. Then he placed Mithu's metal cage between him and Badki. The curious bird sat on the perch, eyeing us, tilting its head left and right. It was cute but it pooped all the time. Thankfully, its droppings didn't stink that much.

Dada lit a candle with a matchstick and held the needle to the flame. "This is for sterilization, to kill germs. Otherwise, the ear holes might get infected and swollen with pus," he explained.

Then, he started narrating a ghost story from his endless repository of tales—a new one gushed out effortlessly like the juice from the tip of a ripe mango.

Between narrating the lines of the story, he asked Badki to feed Mithu a green pepper. As Badki held the pepper to the bird's curved beak and we waited for the story to climax, for the evil spirit to be locked in a bottle by the haunted woman as it did in most of his stories, Dada stretched my sister's lobe and inserted the needle into the marked dot.

"Aahhh!" Badki cried. Our lips trembled, and our eyes moistened.

"Bahadur ladki!" Brave girl. Dada roared a full-throated laugh that drowned Badki's pain and our anxiety.

He cut the thread, tied its ends while blowing on Badki's reddened ear, and gave her another piece of candy. He repeated the process for her other lobe, then for Manjhli and I. Ammi continued sewing in our parents' room. Perhaps she didn't hear our cries in the whirr of her sewing machine.

The parakeet rewarded our bravery by saying its name, Mithu, Mithu, again and again. Despite Dada's persistent training, it hadn't picked up another word.

"Bewaqoof tota!" Foolish parakeet. Dada tapped the birdcage and laughed. We chortled, too.

Then, as we sucked on the lemon candy, Dada announced that on his next pension day, he wouldn't buy sweet laddoos or plastic bangles or rubber dolls for us. Instead, he'd save the money to buy us silver earrings.

"Not fair," we said. We waited for small treats our grandfather brought us once a month on his pension day. But, then, we smiled at the thought of silver glinting in our ears. Many times during the day, we looked at our faces in the mirror—the swollen red lobes, the black thread running through them. Badki said she wanted thin hoops that'd dangle when she walked. Manjhli wanted studs that'd sparkle in the sun. I wanted small rings with flowers carved on them like Ammi's. We asked each other if our piercings hurt. None of us admitted the pain.

At night, my false bravado collapsed. Outside, the clouds that had been circling the sky all day burst open. As did my pain— our pain—which I could feel in the throbbing of my ear and the shaking of my sisters' bodies as they sobbed into the sheets of our slim bed. The clouds rumbled as they emptied their moisture with a plunk-plunk-plunk on the tin shed but we let ours flow in silence.

A Treacherous Fruit

One morning, our cemented courtyard lay covered in wet leaves, twigs, and green mangoes from the tree. It had been a stormy night. We collected the raw mangoes in a tin bucket for Ammi to make achaar. Mango pickles. One of the mangoes we picked from the floor was exceptionally huge—the biggest fruit we'd seen in our lives—and too soft for early summer.

Badki clutched the mango, too big for her palms, and said, "Let's show this to Dada." Manjhli and I followed her.

Inside his room, Dada was kneeling on his patched prayer rug, facing west for his morning prayers—namaz. We waited for him to reach the last part when he raised his index finger, rotated his neck to the right then left, lips moving in prayer, reciting the memorized verses from our holy book, the Quran. His face broke into a wide smile when he saw us. Before he could rise and roll up the prayer mat, Badki placed the giant fruit in his lap.

He picked the mango and examined it carefully. The fruit was longer than his palm, too, extending beyond the length of his fingers. He scratched his flowing beard and said, "Giant fruits, two-headed sheep, double-yolked eggs . . ." Then, after a deep sigh, he added, "Kudrat ke isharey." Signs from nature.

We looked at him, unblinking, expecting more from the reservoir of wisdom he held in the white of his beard, the lines of his face, the folds of skin on his neck.

I observed a gray shadow flit across his face. He had discerned something from the fruit—something disturbing? portentous?—that he didn't disclose it to us. The next moment, he smiled wide, transforming once again into the jovial grandfather we knew.

"Look at the pink here at the tip," he said. "This one will be ready for you all to eat, soon."

Ammi called for us to sweep the courtyard clean of the night's detritus. Dada said he'd keep the mango in a warm place in his room until it ripens—safe from our brothers.

The next day, Abba brought home a loaf of bread and a small packet of butter. Our mouths watered at the aroma of this bakery bread, warm and fresh, very different from the roti Ammi cooked on the flame every day. Ammi cut the bread into four thick slices, smeared them with butter, and called Asif and Salman for a snack. She locked the remaining bread and butter in the cabinet. We licked clean the spoon Ammi had used for spreading the butter.

In the evening, when we went to Dada's room for a story, we noticed his calves had swollen up like the bread loaf our brothers had enjoyed with abandon, discarding the edges, which we had later picked up from the floor and eaten.

We ran to tell Ammi about Dada's legs as she was stirring the saalan pot in the kitchen. She told Abba. He went out to buy some medicine but the tablets that had worked for Dada the last time did not help now. The swelling refused to subside. The skin on Dada's legs became shiny, and deep dimples formed on his calves when we pressed them to comfort him.

A spasm of pain passed over his face but he brushed it away. He grinned and assured us he'd be up with the sun the next day. We believed him. His teeth sparkled white—a reward of his brushing them after every meal. He advised us to do the same but Ammi admonished us for wasting expensive toothpaste. So, we rinsed our mouths with plain water after eating.

The next morning, we peeked into Dada's room, expecting him seated on the mat, bowing his forehead in prayer, but found him lying in his bed instead. His eyes were lined with pain but his lips curved into a narrow smile for us. He said he didn't have the strength to rise and asked us to empty out the plastic cylindrical can which held his collection of nuts and screws, nails and rivets, in all shapes and sizes—his sundry kit for minor repairs around the house. Then, he asked us to leave the room and wait outside for him to call us. We obeyed.

When Dada called, we returned. The stench in the room made us gag and clutch our bellies. Dada pointed to the can on the floor. His smile had evaporated, he didn't lift his eyes to meet ours. Grooves of wrinkles deepened on his forehead. I ran to fetch my dupatta and wrapped it around my face, leaving only a slit open for my eyes, and picked the can up.

The suspension was brown like the milk-less tea Ammi poured for us when our brothers drank every drop of milk in the pot. And the fibrous yellow floating on top looked like mango pulp. I walked slowly, careful not to spill a drop, and emptied the can into the toilet.

That day onward, Dada's room reeked of excrement with an underlying hint of something overripe, on the verge of rotting. Ammi gave us rose incense sticks to light in his room but they did nothing to diffuse the miasma. The parakeet, which chose adamant silence when Dada trained it to speak, now repeated its name, Mithu, Mithu, to cheer him, and perched on the bars along the cage to catch a glimpse of its master. We slid a bowl of soaked daal into its cage but it refused to eat, and only poked at the grains with disinterest.

We took turns emptying the plastic can throughout the day, brought Dada his meals, and huddled on the tattered floor rug as he regaled us, not with the usual ghost and djinn stories, but with tales of prophets from the holy Quran. He taught us an Arabic prayer, Aayat Karima, and asked us to repeat it for the recovery of his health. He said prophet Hazrat Yonus had recited the verse when a giant fish devoured him. Through the power of those lines, he had emerged unharmed from the beast's belly.

We repeated the prayer with every breath as we huddled around Dada all day, leaving him only to sleep in the night.

On the fifth morning we found Dada lying cold in his bed, his hands folded on his chest, a smile on his lips. He looked peaceful, as if the pain he'd endured in the last five days had been scrubbed away. "Allah is kind and merciful," were the words he spoke last evening after he narrated another prophet story and kissed good-night on our foreheads.

We hugged each other and wailed, but Mithu was quiet, sitting in one spot with its eyes shut, head burrowed in its chest, wings limp by the side.

Our brothers and Abba bathed Dada—a death ritual—and wrapped him in a kafan sprinkled with rose ittar. We wept into Dada's chest until it was time for him to go. Ammi pried us away. A light rain fell as our brothers, Abba, and men from the neighborhood carried him out on their shoulders for burial. We sobbed and watched from the door until the janazah procession turned the bend at the end of our alley.

After, to keep our minds busy and to honor Dada, we started cleaning his room. Badki mopped the floor, Manjhli arranged his cans and boxes in rows, and I stripped his bed. Under the cotton mattress and the woven dhurrie, I found the giant mango, wrapped in layers of newspaper. I unpeeled the paper. The fruit was yellow and squishy with brown spots near the top. Its overripe smell nauseated me, the fibrous flesh oozed into my hands.

The parakeet flung into action as if startled awake from a deep slumber. It fluttered its wings, beat its curved beak on the cage, and broke into agitated screams. My sisters stepped away from me as if I were holding a hand grenade. I darted out the door and threw the treacherous fruit into the trash with force, its innards splaying out. Flies flew in and buzzed over it, light reflected by iridescent bodies glinting through wings.

Nights of Silence

After a downpour one evening, the night sky cleared up. It looked like a black dupatta studded with sequins of stars and a milk moon. The subdued fragrance of jasmine flowers planted by Ammi in clay pots mitigated the stench wafting in from the drain outside. We pulled a charpoy into the courtyard and sat on it, trying to make up stories now that Dada wasn't there to narrate them for us. Lying sick in his bed, he'd promised he'd be a star watching over us, always. We looked above at the sky but couldn't tell which star was Dada.

We stopped talking when Ammi walked toward us, carrying the paandan, a metal container holding the ingredients needed to assemble a paan, an edible preparation made using betel leaves and areca nuts. We scooted over to make room for her. She sat on the charpoy, her blue-veined feet resting on the ground.

"Badki, make a paan for me," she said, placing the container on the charpoy. Though all of us helped Ammi in the kitchen with chopping the vegetables and grinding the spices on the stone, Ammi trusted Badki the most with food. Badki enjoyed spending time in the kitchen, sauteing the onions or stirring the saalan so it didn't stick to the bottom of the pot. Manjhli was an expert at sewing buttons and hooks, hemming the cuffs and sleeves of the outfits Ammi sewed for other women. She had a neat, deft way with the needle. I helped Ammi with everything but didn't have a distinguished skill, something I was best at. Now, after Dada died, my sisters said I was good at making up stories and narrating them.

Though Ammi had asked Badki to prepare the paan, Manjhli and I wanted a part in it, too. Badki laid a heart-shaped betel leaf on her palm, dipped oar-like spoons into the little bowls in the paandan, and applied a coating of slaked lime paste to one half. Manjhli painted the other half across the leaf's mid-rib with red catechu paste. I placed pieces of areca nut on the leaf. Ammi plunged a hand into the neckline of her kameez, pulled out a pouch of tobacco, and sprinkled some on the leaf. Then she folded the paan into the size of a pebble and slid it inside her mouth.

Our mother lay back on the charpoy, forearms crossed over her eyes. Slim as she was, she didn't need much space and we squeezed along to the edges to make room for her. Settled in a restful position, she asked, "What kahanis were you girls telling?"

"Chutki is best at telling kahanis, Ammi," Badki said. "She has learned well from Dada."

"Oh, really?" Ammi propped her head on her elbow. She asked me to narrate a story but I giggled and blushed at the sudden attention.

"Let me try telling one kahani, then," Ammi said.

"Yes, yes, Ammi!" We let out a burst of joy and clapped our hands in anticipation.

We heard Abba clear his throat twice, a sign for us to be quiet and not disturb our brothers in their studies. Sometimes, when we talked excitedly or played akkad-bakkad in our room, Abba stormed in and hung his belt on the wall peg as a warning, but he had never struck us. There was also this fact we knew about our brothers that Abba didn't: they spent more time leafing through comic books, drawing funny figures, and flying paper airplanes than they did studying.

Ammi began the story of an infant girl born in winter who cried all night and all day despite being dressed in warm cotton-wool layers and swaddled in flannel blankets. Hours of rocking and multiple attempts of offering her the breast by the mother did not calm the infant. The father berated the mother for giving

17

birth to a kambakht baby.

After this, Ammi paused as if to decide what happened next or to change her story. We waited.

"One night the baby cried and cried without a pause and the father ordered the mother to visit the midwife the next morning for some oleander poison . . ." her lips quivered, ". . . to silence the infant."

"Did she?" I asked, hoping the baby girl was safe.

"The mother undressed the baby girl down to her skin, took her out into the cold night, and whispered something in her ear. The baby stopped crying at night. Not a peep. Only during the day when the father was out at the fields did she let her voice out of her body."

"What did the mother tell the baby?" I asked.

Ammi answered in a faint snore. The paan, a little bulge under her cheek, releasing tobacco juices into her throat, had lulled her to sleep. I fetched a pillow and placed it under her head. Manjhli turned the lone light bulb off, and we massaged Ammi's legs and feet. She moaned as her limbs released some of their weariness.

Green-gray frogs croaked and hopped out from their hiding spots as if they knew they were safe with us. Our brothers liked to chase the poor creatures, crush them with bricks, and then dry their bodies to crisps in the sun. We hated their game of torture and death.

We looked up at the sky. This time, one star directly above us shone unmistakably brighter than the others. "Dada!" we whispered. Fireflies danced around the jasmine pots, mangoes hung like silver balls on the tree, Ammi's skin felt warm and soft under our fingers. We could have sat in the courtyard all night but a sheet of gray cloud soon shrouded the sky.

The rain came in intermittent drops, a fat one landing on Ammi's cheek. She opened her eyes and continued with the story as if she hadn't dozed off in the middle of it, "No girl should ever be birthed in winter." Then, she ran a palm over our heads. "But a woman should have daughters to make her a paan and massage her legs."

She rose from the charpoy, a hand pressed to her kneecap, her face contorting with pain. I placed slippers on her feet and she shuffled inside. We pulled the cot under the shed and went inside, too.

We lay along the width of our bed—the only arrangement that worked to fit the three of us on the narrow frame—and, like every night, we heard Ammi's glass bangles and Abba's grunts through the thin wall separating our room from theirs. Never a sound from Ammi. And I thought of the girl, born in winter, threatened into nights of silence.

Ramadan

The generous rains that year made the day-long fasts without a drop of water or a grain of food during the month of Ramadan tolerable. Although our bellies roiled from hunger, our lips didn't crack, our tongues didn't parch. We could feel the raindrops coating our tongues, trickling down our mouths, moistening our throats.

Abba didn't fast, and neither did our brothers. Ammi instructed us to observe Ramadan, a key practice of Islam, otherwise our future husbands would call us kafirs and blame our unholy up-bringing for misfortunes that might fall on our marital homes.

After we broke our fast at sunset with sweet dates and water, Ammi poured more water for us to drink. A pang rose in our guts. We missed Dada and the half liter of milk he bought for us every day in the month of Ramadan. But, we yearned for his gentle presence, his warm kindness, more than the sweetness of milk. His laughter echoed in our ears until the sound of azaan, the call for prayer, rang out across terraces and courtyards. We washed down the lumps in our throats with water.

"Women carry the burden of appeasing the seen and the un-seen, the present and the future," Ammi used to say. After Dada's death, something had changed shape inside Ammi. She talked to us more, even cared for us a little more, maybe.

Though the Ramadan days without food were hard, we looked forward to the pre-dawn meal sehri because Ammi cooked fresh parathas in ghee to give us strength to last the long, hungry day. That was a meal Ammi prepared especially for us, not a leftover after our brothers had eaten. The aroma entered our nostrils and tickled our tongues, but we controlled ourselves and didn't gorge on the food. Instead, we chewed slowly, savoring each bite lubricated by our mother's love, basking in each moment of her undivided attention while Abba and our brothers slept until the sun shone on the mango tree outside.

One morning, after sehri, as we lay awake in our narrow bed, Badki suggested we call random people on the phone, just for fun. The telephone was installed recently at our house—a black, toad-like appliance, sitting on a wooden stool in the living room. We used to watch Asif and Salman dial their friends' numbers and say "Hello." They shooed us away but we stood outside and eavesdropped. They whispered curse words like haraami, kamina into the phone and guffawed at their own insolence.

I tiptoed into the living room, pulled the telephone and the book lying beside it into our room, and shut the door. In the streetlight streaming in through the window, our leader Badki looked at the numbers in the book, found the matching shapes on the dialer, and twirled them as we'd seen our brothers do. We huddled close to the receiver and heard the tring-tring before a man picked up and barked an angry "Hello," into our ears. Badki put the phone down, her fingers trembling. Manjhli tried next but couldn't muster the courage to talk when someone answered the ring. We decided to try again the next night.

In preparation for the anonymous calls, we practiced modulating our voices to sound different than our normal selves although not many outside the family had heard our voices. Even our Abba couldn't discern our voices from one other. Maybe he could recognize a voice as one of ours, but he definitely wouldn't know to which one of us it belonged. For him, everything about us was interchangeable.

I practiced speaking like the lady doctor Doctorni who visited us for vaccinations, polio drops, and brought vitamins for Ammi. She was an elegant lady, dressed in a starched sari, hair wound up in a high bun, a stethoscope dangling around her neck. I was in awe of her elegance and authority, watching her with wide eyes on each encounter. I stretched the "o" sound into "ooo" like she did.

The next day, after sehri, I volunteered to make the phone calls. When a kind-voiced woman answered, I whispered "Hel-looo," with a confidence that matched Doctorni's. The woman on the phone spoke at length about how she'd cooked biryani in the evening, how her husband said it was too salty and burnt, ordered her to apologize and cook a fresh pot, though she'd been the one fasting all day.

We were so engrossed in the woman's woes that we didn't notice when Ammi slipped into our room. After I put the receiver down, she said, "And who are we calling next?" A slant of light fell on her face and her bow-shaped lips curved into a smile. Before we could reply, she snuggled in with us and we made more calls, clamping our mouths with our hands to stifle the laughter, reminding each other of Abba's belt that he hung in our room to warn us when we made noise. Luckily he was in a deep sleep at that hour, his loud snores masking our whispers.

We continued the prank calls every morning during Ramadan and talked only when a woman answered the ring. Sometimes, we connected to some neighborhood women we knew. We didn't reveal our identity and they opened their guarded hearts to us. For us, it was pure joy. For the women we called, it was a vent for grievances. For Ammi, I imagined it was a reprieve from her duties of taking care of a large family, cooking tall stacks of rotis while fasting.

On the day of Eid, the holiday at the end of Ramadan, women from the neighborhood came to greet Ammi. As we served them bowls of sweet seviyan, we heard them talk about a bunch of young girls—fun-seeking but kind-hearted—calling their houses after sehri.

Ammi scrunched up her face and said, "Don't know why parents let their children use the telephone like a toy. Bad times, sisters." Then, she tore her eyes from the women and shot us a mischievous look.

We ran outside and giggled. The rain came on, a light drizzle transforming into a torrent, and we laughed heartily, the fat drops muffling the sound of our glee.

A Sore Symphony

The day we'd not forget all our lives started with a sunny morning that gave way to a soft but persistent drizzle by noon. We rushed to pull our brothers' school pants and shirts from the clothesline in the courtyard and hang them in the shade to dry. Otherwise, the clothes would smell musty and our brothers would grumble and complain about our carelessness. The tinkle of Ammi's glass bangles as she rolled out rotis in the kitchen and laid them on the griddle broke the hiss of falling water.

Then, we heard a thud in the kitchen, followed by silence. We looked at each other, our eyes filled with fear and worry. We heaped the damp clothes onto the charpoy and rushed to check on Ammi. Our mother was lying on the floor, her hands dusted with wheat flour, a stream of sweat running down her hairline, a broken glass bangle poking into the skin of her inner wrist. I turned the kerosene stove off, Badki placed Ammi's head in her lap, and Manjhli sprinkled her face with water. Ammi opened her eyes for half a second before her eyelids dropped again.

I tied together the ends of my dupatta to prevent it from flying away and ran to the dispensary to fetch Doctorni. By the time I returned with the lady doctor, my sisters had moved Ammi to the bed and were fanning her face with a punkah—the electricity had gone out. Doctorni felt for Ammi's pulse and placed the silver disc of the stethoscope on Ammi's chest. After listening to Ammi's heartbeat, she rolled up our mother's sleeve, pulled out a syringe from her bag, and plunged a needle into her skinny arm. Within seconds, Ammi's eyelids fluttered open.

"Another baby!" the doctor shook her head in disbelief and gave Ammi an accusatory look. "I told you, sister, you have no material to build more bones, no strength to birth more humans.

24

Believe me, I know. Look at your pale skin and dull eyes."

Ammi looked at the floor in deep thought and asked us to leave the room. We obeyed and hovered outside, our ears pressed to the wall, but couldn't grasp a word of the hushed conversation between the two women.

That afternoon, we asked Ammi to take araam. Rest. When Asif and Salman returned from school, we served them lunch that Ammi had finished cooking before she fainted. They asked for more and more of the meat saalan until a few fleshless bones were left in the pot for us.

In the evening, Abba returned from work. As he slipped his shoes off, he called out for Ammi to make chai. Badki told him she'd make it because Ammi was sleeping. She was unwell. He mumbled something under his breath and sat in a chair under the asbestos awning outside the kitchen, flipping the newspaper. He didn't bother to check on Ammi or even ask us about her health. Having grown up with only brothers and a biased mother, per-haps the idea of taking care of a woman never crossed his mind. Badki set a pot on the stove for chai but the milk was locked inside the wire-meshed cabinet.

We went inside to ask Ammi but she was snoring softly. Man-jhli untied the keys from the drawstring of Ammi's salwar, taking great care not to disturb her. That day, for the first time in our lives, we had all the milk to ourselves, but none of us wanted a drop from the ocean in front of us.

Badki brought chai for Abba in his large white mug, the biggest in the house. Abba took a sip and complained the drink wasn't warm enough. When Badki reheated it, the chai took on an ugly, wet-mud color. Abba held the cup away at an arm's length. "What's this?" he yelled at Badki. "Kadva zehar?" Bitter poison. His eyes flashed with anger, his hands quivered with rage.

"I'll make a good one, Abba," Badki mumbled and ran into the kitchen.

Abba crushed the newspaper in his big hands and threw it on the floor, grumbling how there wasn't even a moment of joy in this house full of worthless girls.

After some time, Ammi called for us, "Badki, Manjhli, Chutki . . ." in a weak voice and we scuttled to her. Ammi wrapped an arm around Badki's shoulder and tried to rise from the bed but fell back into the thin mattress. She said her legs felt soft like cooked bone marrow, too weak to bear her weight, and it was already time to prepare dinner. We requested her to give us instructions.

Despite Manjhli and I helping her with chopping or washing the vegetables, grinding spices on the grindstone, and Badki stir-frying the onions, Ammi hadn't allowed us to cook a meal independently. Abba liked his food prepared exactly in his mother's way that Ammi had adopted. He wouldn't allow any deviation from the familiar tastes he had grown up with. Ammi said after marriage she had to unlearn the cooking methods and recipes she had observed in her mother's kitchen, had to forget the flavors of her childhood.

Ammi gave us directions to prepare a simple meal: daal tempered with garlic, served with roti and rice. "Preparing a meat dish will be complicated for you," she said. "It requires skill and experience."

Badki rolled out and cooked the rotis, Manjhli tempered the daal, and I boiled the rice. When we served the dinner to our brothers, they mocked the watery daal and threw pieces of roti at each other. After they left the kitchen, we cleared the mess before Abba sat down to eat on his low stool. Badki fanned his face with the punkah. A few bites in, he pushed the plate away and said, "Pour some milk and sugar over the rice for me. An azaab of a meal, this is, after a day's hard work."

26

We held our breaths as Abba's anger rose palpably with each morsel of the sugared rice. A thick vein pulsated in his temple. Finally, he gulped down a glass of water, kicked the stool out of the way, and stomped out saying, "No man deserves this food!"

The swishing of his kurta as he walked past us, the draft of air displaced by the movement made us shiver. The hair on our bodies stood erect. We rubbed our palms to generate some heat, then served two rotis, a bowl of daal, and a heap of rice on a plate for Ammi and took it to her. She smiled and ate without a word, looking at a spot on the wall where the plaster was swollen and peeling because of the dampness caused by the rain.

That night, after washing the dishes and sweeping the kitchen, we lay quiet, worried about Ammi's health, thinking about the doctor's concern, and dreading the thought of a new baby. We barely had enough to eat. We heard Asif and Salman laughing and snorting in their room. Asif said aloud, making sure we could hear, "The daal was a dirty pond with no fish." Salman shouted, "And the rotis were maps of continents yet to be discovered and printed in geography books." Then, the pun at us turned into a scuffle. We heard them wrestling each other for packets of Parle-G biscuits they kept in their room to snack on while studying.

Abba's heavy steps emerged from our parents' room and deflected towards our brothers' room. He commanded Asif and Salman to stop fighting and get back to studying and chided them softly for not doing enough mehnat. Hard work. "Let me at least sleep in peace," he added before leaving. "Didn't even have a decent morsel on this cursed day."

Our brothers chimed in, "Yes, Abba, we are hungry, too. We can't study on a khaali pet." Empty stomach.

"All because of these kambakht women. They need a lesson," Abba flounced back into our parent's room and then towards ours, his feet heavy on the floor, something metallic jangling with his step. The belt.

Except this time he did not hang it on the peg as a warning for us.

"Useless girls!" he stormed in and whipped the buckled lash on the wall of our room. His anger filled the space and a spike of cold fear ran through us. Badki flipped from her back to her belly, Manjhli and I followed her cue. The first lash struck our backs, a shock that tore our skin, crept into our bones.

We screamed and screamed, and said repeatedly, "Maaf kar do Abba." Please forgive us. The apology unlocked more of his fury and perhaps his mind justified the punishment he meted out to us. The insipid chai, the sugared rice, our brothers' complaints had roused the demon in him like never before. He struck and yelled. "Only good for eating, you bitches! Damn your mother for giving me girl after girl and keeping each one alive."

Abba's words cut deeper than the leather belt. It was no secret that Abba resented us but this was another level of insult and injury, a blow at our existence. Ammi stumbled into our room, still weak, holding onto the doors and walls, and flung her thin frame over our bodies. That didn't stop Abba's lashes. If anything, it only escalated his fury.

He went on to relieve his pent-up aggression against Ammi. "Your womb is cursed, woman," he shouted at her. "I should have listened to my Ma and sent you back long ago, should have given you a talaaq." Divorce.

"Ammi, you go, please," we said between cries as Abba whipped us, but our mother didn't budge or utter an "Aah." We, too, stopped screaming and absorbed the blows. Abba threw the belt on the floor and left, yelling, "Maro, tum sab!" Die, you all.

We clutched Ammi and sobbed silently, wiping each other's snot and tears with dupattas. Outside, no thunder, no clouds, as if the universe was an audience to our sore symphony. We were the drops that fell that night.

Leaving Home

Ammi woke us up late in the morning. The house lay very quiet—no pitter-patter of raindrops, no rumbling of clouds, no wind slamming the doors. Abba had left for work and our brothers for school. Sunlight from the window formed a golden pool at our feet. Our clothes were stained golden, too, by the turmeric paste Ammi applied to our belt injuries—and we to hers—last night.

The smell of burnt milk hung in the air. Ammi must have been really distracted to let the milk boil over. Frugal as she was, she wouldn't waste a drop, otherwise.

The night had healed us. Our wounds didn't sting anymore. Ammi's face wasn't paper-pale like the day before when she'd fainted. Her pupils shone but underneath the sunlight dancing in her eyes, lurked something different—something steely.

She asked us to call her mother, our Naani, who had had a phone installed at her place, recently. Naani wrote about it in a letter that Asif had read out aloud. Our grandmother could read and write. Ammi told us she had attended night school after her husband—the grandfather we never met—passed away.

I dialed Naani's number that Salman had written in green ink on the first page of the phonebook. She answered on the first ring, her voice soothing like the first sip of water at the break of a fast during Ramadan. Because long-distance calls were expensive, Ammi kept the conversation brief and urged Naani to visit soon, without telling her about the last night. Then, she asked us to collect all our clothes and arrange them in bundles.

"Ammi, are we going somewhere?" Badki asked.

Ammi didn't reply. We made three heaps of our faded clothes, mine the most worn-out because they passed from Badki to Manjhli to me, and tied each one up separately in old dupattas with frayed edges.

Naani arrived the following day, a cabbage-green chaddar wrapped around her head and torso, a bag of apples balanced in the crook of her left elbow, a surahi—earthen pot of water—in her right hand. Our grandmother had the same face as Ammi—the high forehead, the saucer eyes, the sharp nose, the elegant bone structure—but her cheeks were full and rosy while Ammi's were sunken and sallow. Ammi rushed into her mother's arms and wept inconsolably, hiccupping like a child.

"Take my daughters with you, Ma," Ammi said, wiping her nose on her sleeve. "I can't shield them. I failed." She started crying again.

We told our grandmother about Abba's explosive rage last night, the belt lashes, Ammi's illness, and Doctorni's words. She puckered her mouth with worry, pulled out a tasbih from her pocket, and thumbed the white beads.

"Ya, Allah! Another baby?" She said, after completing a round of quick prayers. The creases around her eyes became visible.

"Yes . . . due in winter . . . the potion I use failed this time . . ." Ammi said, and then with a confidence that belied her trembling voice, "But I'll take care of it with Doctorni's help."

Naani kissed Ammi's forehead. "Allah, reham kar." God, have mercy.

"Why am I not strong like you, Ma? Why can't I whisper something into my daughters' ears to protect them . . . like you did that winter night when I was a baby?"

"It was Allah who spoke to you that winter. I was His voice. As for my strength, it came after your Abba died. You were already married but I had to fend for your two younger sisters. Before, I was a paper kite, my string in your Abba's hands. After, I became a bird, hopping about, flying, gathering food to feed my daughters."

31

"How are my Safina and Zoya?" Ammi asked with a cheer in her voice as she spoke her sisters' names.

"Oh, they're well. Still refuse to marry, and I don't force them. They're learning to read and write from a social worker lady who comes home to teach them. Too embarrassed to take night classes, those girls."

"We want to read and write too, Naani!" I squealed. "Can we?"

"Insha'allah," Naani said. If Allah wills it. "The room on my terrace is occupied by pigeons, right now. I'll ask Safina and Zoya to clean it up for you all. You can sleep there."

"But, Ma, will you have enough to feed my girls?" Ammi asked. "Though they eat like sparrows, really."

"Your father's little property provides enough to get by. There's that small mango orchard that yields income in the summer. Plus, the social worker lady promised to register me for a welfare scheme to start some kind of home business—pickles, papads, candles . . ."

"We'll make papads with you, Naani," Badki said, and we wrapped our arms around our grandmother's girth, her hips and waist cushiony, at least two times as wide as our mother's.

"Ammi, you come with us, too," I said. "Please?"

"Who will cook for your brothers and Abba, then?" she said, looking at a spot beyond my shoulder, a tremor creeping into her voice. "I have my own kismet. You all, go, make your lives better."

And, just like that, after sobbing Khuda Hafiz into Ammi's cotton kameez, we stepped out of the house, open-toed plastic sandals strapped to our feet, bundles of clothes wrapped in dupattas balanced on our heads, leaving behind a life that could have become only more painful—of this we were certain. A truth that was unwise to ignore, even at that age.

Before turning the bend at the end of our alley, I paused and looked back. Ammi stood with her dupatta held to her mouth, leaning against the swollen door washed almost naked of the blue paint, patched in places with aluminum scraps. The mango tree peeked over the wall, looking mournful, the fruits and leaves static.

Naani urged us to walk faster or we'd miss the train to her town. We waved to Ammi. She raised a hand slowly as if it weighed at least five kilograms. Manjhli swiveled around but our grandmother held her arm.

We walked on. Above us, the sky stretched clear and wide. Would our sky remember us or would it just not care—chameleon that it was, changing colors and moods many times a day. Would Naani's sky be ink-blue or iron-gray, smattered with pebbly clouds or covered with puffy cotton ball ones?

Would Dada, looking down from the strip of sky above our courtyard worry about not finding us here? Would he ask Allah's angels, farishtey, about us? Would they help him locate us like they came to the aid of the prophets in Quran?

A rainbow arched in the sky. That was impossible on such a dry day. I looked again, puzzled, and it had vanished. My mind was already inventing colors, painting a new sky for us.

Moradabad Station

It was our first time on a train. We reveled in the sights of rice fields, the cows tottering in pastures, the smell of tube-well water cascading into furrows, the rhythmic sound of the iron wheels on tracks and the nudge of the air of freedom enveloping us. The sky, clear and sunny as the train pulled out from our town, turned pencil gray as we crossed the countryside.

Our brothers traveled, sometimes, for school trips. Upon return, they drew pictures of trains and ran around the house, singing "choo-choo," and shouting "chai, chai," to mimic the tea vendors at the platforms. We played pretend-train by placing our brothers' chairs back to back in a line and covering them with an old bedsheet, each chair a compartment. Badki, the driver, sat on the first seat and made choo-choo sounds.

The sky started leaking. We pressed our faces to the window bars to feel the plink-plonk on our cheeks, stretched our palms out to catch the rupee-sized drops. The rain, as if eager to drench us, slanted in with the wind and Naani pulled the glass screens over the window.

After two stations, the clouds cleared away. It was hot and humid in the second-class compartment. We drank cool water from Naani's earthen surahi. She bought us treats—puffed pooris, cut cucumber, spicy samosas—from vendors who hopped in and out when the train stopped, woven baskets of snacks balanced on their heads, blackened kettles filled with chai, dangling from their arms.

The abundance of food and the variety of scenes that spilled like seeds—cornstalks glistening in sunlight, shirtless boys bathing under tube wells, buffaloes soaking in swamps, oxen ploughing the fields, women pressing cow-dung cakes on mud walls—

entranced us. None of us mentioned home or Ammi. Just like that, we'd changed colors.

Soon, the surahi was empty and none of the vendors aboard were selling water. At the next station, where the row of faucets on the platform was right outside our window, Naani asked Badki to refill the pot. We watched from between the window bars as Badki turned the faucet clockwise like we did at our home, but no water came. She looked sideways at the man filling a jug beside her, observed, and pressed the faucet at the top. Out gushed a stream of water. After she filled the surahi, Badki splashed her face and waved at us. Our grandmother signaled for her to hurry back in.

We guzzled the cool water and in no time the pot was empty again. Naani said the next refill would be at Moradabad where the train stopped for a good twenty minutes. I volunteered. Naani said it was best Badki did the refill because she was the tallest but eventually gave in to my insistence when I showed her how tall I was by standing on my toes.

Moradabad being a bigger station, a crowd thronged the row of faucets fixed on a low wall. It took me a while to jostle my way to the front. I filled the pot and lifted it up for my sisters to see as if I'd won us a trophy. Then, the station master's bell rang—an indication for the train to start moving, Naani had explained.

I rushed back to the door of our compartment, packed with men trying to squeeze in. "Hato, tum sab!" I shouted. Move, you all. But, no one listened. I kneed and elbowed and managed to slide my foot inside the coach right before the wheels started rolling. Pressed between men, reaching little higher than their elbows, I moved forward in the compartment like a stone tossed along by water—a gushing river of shirts and kurtas, muslin and polyester, mustaches and beards, tobacco and sweat.

A groping hand slid under my dupatta and two rough fingers pinched the hard nub, the slight bump on the left of my chest, then slid to the right. Needles of pain shot through my body. A shriek rose to my throat but I swallowed it, remembering how Abba pelted us harder with his belt when we screamed. I drew strength from every corner of my body to absorb the pain; my hands trembled around the surahi but I held on to it for my sisters, thirsty and waiting for water.

On reaching our corner, I handed the pot to Manjhli, and sank into the seat, away from the window, closer to Naani, my arms crossed over my chest, fists curled and buried under my armpits. My body clenched to choke the sobs, hold them inside. It hurt so bad I thought my body would split. And I realized that's why clouds groaned when holding in the rains.

At Naani's House

It was an orange-mauve evening on the verge of merging into twilight gray when we alighted from the rickshaw at Naani's house, a place bigger than ours, with two entrances—a porched door that led into the rooms, and a side one that opened into the courtyard like our blue door, only hers wasn't patched with aluminum.

Our two aunts, Safina Khala and Zoya Khala, opened the side door, welcomed us with brief hugs and "aao, aao,"—welcome—but their voices lacked the warmth I'd expected. Naani had called them from our house about our arrival. Though they weren't twins, they looked exactly like each other, and like Ammi—the same face cut and height but they had more flesh on their bones, a glow of health on their cheeks. Safina Khala was elder to Zoya Khala and slightly plumper in the middle.

They showed us our terrace room upstairs which they had swept and mopped in preparation for our arrival but the air inside still smelled faintly of pigeon droppings. There was no bed or any other furniture in the room. Our aunts had spread cottonwool mattresses on the floor, covered them with faded sheets that looked soft and comfortable.

"Fold the sheets and roll up the mattresses before you leave the room every morning," Safina Khala said. "We like to maintain a tidy house," Zoya Khala added. With that they laid down a code of conduct—we were to follow their instruction here.

The next day, our routine started to take shape. Badki was assigned to help with chai preparation for breakfast, Manjhli to sweep away the roti crumbs after, and I to wash the dishes. After we completed our chores, the social worker lady Didi arrived, dressed in a cotton sari draped around her tall frame, hair rolled into a tight bun, just like our Doctorni back home. Naani requested Didi to teach us the Hindi and English alphabet; she smiled kindly at us.

I was faster and more interested than my sisters in learning. While Badki and Manjhli took naps in the afternoon, I pored over our aunts' books and practiced writing in the single-ruled notebooks our grandmother had bought for us. Didi was impressed by my progress and awarded me a pencil with a scented pink eraser attached at its end. I passed it to my sisters and they held it to their noses, inhaling the jasmine smell that reminded us of Ammi's potted flowers that she tended with care, pruning and watering them regularly.

One week after we arrived, Naani gathered us up and called Ammi. "Beti, how are you?" she said into the phone. Long-distance calls were expensive, so she came to the point quickly. "Were you able to take care of . . . the baby?" We couldn't hear what Ammi said but watched Naani's face for cues. She took a deep breath and said, "That's for the best. Don't blame yourself, and eat better. Add some flesh to the sparrow-like bones."

We looked at each other and an unspoken understanding passed through our eyes. Naani passed the phone to us, one by one. Badki spoke about how she was learning to cook biryani from Naani, Manjhli told about the tiny clothes she was sewing for the doll she'd found in the store. On my turn, my eyes misted over when Ammi said "My little Chutki," in a voice glazed with all the love she had withheld from us for years. I blinked away the tears and told her I could now write simple words and had earned a prize from our teacher, too. "Shabash," Ammi said. Well done.

One day, a rickshawallah knocked at Naani's house and unloaded two baskets of small but ripe mangoes at the doorstep. Our grandmother told us those were the damaged fruits from her orchard, ones that were unfit for the market because they had fallen off the branches and gotten bruised, or were nibbled at by birds.

"We'll have fun today," Naani's eyes shone like a little girl's. "Be ready, my children." Before we could ask more, she slipped on her canvas shoes and went out the door into the alleys of the neighborhood. Our aunts asked us to dress in the oldest, most threadbare clothes we had. Although all our kameezes were old, we picked out ones that had rips or holes that Ammi had darned with her deft fingers.

That afternoon, about ten women from the neighborhood came in, all dressed in old clothes, and gathered around the mango baskets arranged in the center of the courtyard by our aunts. "Shuru karo!" Naani said. Begin.

The women dug their arms up to their elbows into the basket to grab the softest mangoes that they threw at each other, the ripe fruit bursting open like egg yolks on clothes and skin. They smeared the golden pulp over each other's faces and necks and squeezed sweet juice into each other's hair. Looked like it was a game they knew well, that they played every mango season. Peals of laughter and an appetizing aroma filled the air.

The three of us stood against the wall, unsure what to do. Naani signaled us to come forward. Badki and Manjhli went ahead but I stood rooted to my spot. My body stiffened at the sight of the bodies jostling against each other, and a knot twisted in my stomach. The horrific vision etched in my brain appeared again. I had not been able to erase it. It popped up when I closed my eyes in the night—the train compartment packed with bodies, a man's hand groping me as I moved forward clutching the surahi.

My arms rose of their own volition and crossed over my chest, fists burying themselves in my armpits. Goosebumps flared up like tiny hills on my skin. Safina Khala yelled, "Chutki, why are you standing there like an officer? Are you supervising every-one?" Zoya Khala signaled me to join. My ears burned, and I felt all eyes were staring at me, but I didn't budge.

Naani tore out of the jolly group toward me and applied some mango pulp to my cheeks with gentle fingers. My tongue flicked out, trying to taste the sweetness. She held out a yellow mango with a brown scar for me, and I let my arms fall away from my chest. I crushed the fruit and smeared the pulp on my grand-mother's bare arms. She held my hand and pulled me into the center amidst the bubbly women.

My body shed its inhibition and fear, knowing I was safe and protected here. I mingled with the women, covering them with the sticky fruit, partaking in the sweet play. We were happy women, free women, shouting-in-glee women.

A Rain Mutiny

The eventful life-changing summer was coming to a close. Some mornings and evenings, we could feel a nip of autumn in the air, but Naani's house was warmer than ours at this time of the year—not just temperature-wise.

Our days were consumed with chores and our education. I had already progressed to the English alphabet. Naani promised to enroll us in a school after we'd learned basic reading and writing. She even bought us jute bags and we paraded with those slung on our shoulders like the college students back home. Naani had signed papers to start the home business of making mango achaar, and we were looking forward to that for another reason—she would buy us silver earrings after that income from the new venture started flowing in.

At night, after drinking half cups of sweet milk, savoring each sip, and licking our milk mustaches, we sat on the terrace around our grandmother, listening to her stories of defying women, brave women, mystical women with supernatural powers. Anytime she mentioned a ghost, we looked up in the sky, and a star shone ten times brighter, obscuring the others. We knew Dada had found us.

One early morning, it rained hard as if a giant faucet had been turned on in the sky. Water pooled on the terrace outside our room. The plastic slippers we'd left outside bobbed up and down like paper boats. We fished them out and went downstairs to help our aunts with breakfast preparation but found them in the tin shed outside the kitchen, looking at the curtains of rain falling around them, sideways.

"How beautiful!" our aunts pointed at the pink-yellow pomegranates nodding on the tree in the courtyard as if to shake off the raindrops. But the air, fresh at first, fouled up as water from outside seeped under the side door into the courtyard. Exactly like it did at our house. Stinky water, sneaky water. We thought of Ammi, battling the floods by herself, and guilt coursed through us, the guilt of leaving her. I hoped Asif and Salman were helping her drain the water out of the house.

"Badki, Manjhli, Chutki, aao. Let's push the damn water out," our aunts' call spurred us into action. We rolled up our salwar cuffs, grabbed the brooms, our weapons against the encroaching water, and followed our aunts, who marched ahead, armed with stick mops.

As soon as Safina Khala unlatched the side door, a dog growled. We looked in the direction of the sound—a female, a mother, lay on the raised, covered porch outside the main door, a few feet from the side door. Puppies, five of them, mud-brown, suckled at the dog's teats.

Safina Khala yelled, "Saali Kutiya!" Damned bitch. She and Zoya Khala raised the mops above their heads to scare the dog away. She stared back, defiant. "Fetch a pail, girls, throw cold water on the bitch before she and the pups start shitting and pissing here," Zoya Khala commanded.

The dog rose into a crouched position, the puppies holding tight to her stretched teats. Her eyes, flaring with fear now, flicked from our aunts to us. At that moment, the ridicule and insult we suffered back home darted through our minds: our brothers, even their rickshawallah, shooing us away like we were stray dogs, Abba calling us bitches as he struck us, that fateful night. The aches began to flare. The bitter humiliation and indignation layered in the pits of our stomachs rose up to the backs of our throats.

"Badki, Manjhli, Chutki, get moving!" our aunts commanded. "Scare away these beasts. What are you waiting for?"

We looked at each other, expecting one of us to do something about our aunts' orders. Badki ran inside, fetched a stale roti from the kitchen, and threw it to the dog. She ducked at first, doubting our intention, then gobbled down the bread.

"What are you doing, girls?" our aunts shouted. "These dogs will turn your Naani's porch into a stinking pakhana!"

The dog whimpered. A plea.

Manjhli brought discarded bones from last night's meal, hurled them at the dog. The animal tore away the remnants of flesh with her teeth, licked the bones clean. I flung an empty burlap rice sack from the storeroom at the dog. She caught the cloth in her mouth and pulled it over the shivering puppies. They mewled.

"Tauba, tauba!" Oh My God. Our aunts hissed in disgust and stomped inside, leaving us the chore of draining the dirty water. We didn't mind it, we did it almost every day at our home. That day, we just wanted the dogs to rest in a dry shelter.

The dog looked at us with gratitude, then rested her head on the floor and closed her eyes in peace. The puppies curled up under the burlap sack. We held each other's hands in solidarity.

As we drained the courtyard, the rain relented and the sun broke through the clouds. "Look, a rainbow!" my sisters pointed at the multi-colored arc on the patch of sky above the pomegranate tree. What my eyes saw was not one but three colorful arches, one above the other, crowning the tree. I rubbed my eyes, shook my head out of its imagination, and looked again. One splash, a brushstroke of seven colors, still hung there. And, it was enough.

Free Birds

Every week, we used to wait for Friday mid-morning, the time our grandmother had allocated to call Ammi, when she'd be alone after our brothers and Abba left for the day. Naani said Friday was a good day, a sacred day blessed by Allah. While waiting for the time of the call, we made mental notes of the highlights we wanted to share with our mother.

After the mango festival, Badki told Ammi about the fun we had in Naani's courtyard, playing with the neighbors and laughing out aloud with them.

"It must be a new gathering your Naani is organizing now," Ammi said with nostalgia and longing. "Wasn't a part of my bachpan." Childhood.

We huddled close, our ears pressed to the telephone receiver as each one of us took turns talking to Ammi. She went on to say she was glad we had a good time with the women, but her voice lacked the vigor and excitement we thought she reserved for our calls. When I asked about her health, Ammi said she'd been sick with malaria for the last four-five days, and was still weak. My ears burned, and I looked at my sisters. They had heard, too. We all lowered our eyes to the floor, ashamed at our frolicking with our grandmother, aunts, and other women when our mother was burning with fever back home.

Ammi perked her voice up, asked us not to worry, and said our brothers had taken care of her illness. Salman had placed wet cotton strips on her forehead to reduce the fever; Asif had heated up milk for her and also cooked a simple meal of khichadi on her instruction. We burst into smiles and clapped our hands in joy. My chest puffed up in pride.

I was holding a secret in the deepest corner of my heart. I had written a letter in my awkward handwriting and misspelled words to Asif and Salman, and asked Naani to post it, requesting her not to tell anyone. In the note, I'd urged my brothers to take care of Ammi, to help her around the house, especially in pushing the rainwater away from the courtyard. They had not replied, so I guessed they would have ripped the letter into pieces or made an airplane or a boat out of it. The only thing they would have paid any attention to would be my misspellings. But, now, I was convinced my words had hit their hearts.

Manjhli asked Ammi about Mithu. Ammi said the bird repeated its name, again and again, to entertain Ammi when she was sick like it did when Dada was bed-ridden. After Ammi's fever subsided and she was back on her feet, she opened up the square door of Mithu's cage. It hopped out, followed Ammi to the kitchen, and sat on the low spice rack. Then, it fluttered its wings and flew up to the courtyard wall where it perched for a long time before soaring higher, drawn to the call of free birds.

Though we were happy for Mithu's freedom, when we sat on the terrace, late in the afternoon, to catch some breeze, we discussed if the bird would be alright. We hoped it had not fallen prey to a predator. Badki and Manjhli puckered their faces and furrowed their brows.

"Don't know where Mithu would be," Manjhli said, her eyes sad and tinted bronze in the light of the dying sun.

"Maybe Dada will look over Mithu," Badki said, holding her hand to her face as a shade against the late-afternoon brilliance. "I hope he finds his pet bird."

I said we'd miss Mithu's excited screeches and urgent scampering inside the cage when we visited home. Naani had promised to take us for a short trip on the holiday of Eid, which was still five months away.

The sound of azaan—the call for evening prayer—rang out

from the loudspeaker at the neighborhood mosque, and we covered our heads with dupattas in reverence as Naani had taught us. The last rays of the sun gilded the parapet wall around us and accentuated the worried expression on my sisters' faces. Then, the deep vermilion in the cloudless sky scattered into smudges of pink, and we saw a string of birds fringing the arc of the sun. We intertwined our fingers and smiled.

Acknowledgements

No words can express my gratitude to my parents, Abi and Ammi, for their sacrifices, big and small, to provide the best education possible to me, without which my writing would not have existed. To Abi for his unwavering belief in me, for his steadfast support towards all my endeavors. I regret not having written this book earlier, regret not watching Abi smile as he would have when turning the pages. To Ammi, my rock and inspiration. Every conversation with you kindles in me a renewed resolve to write. To my brothers and sisters, my lifelong cheerleaders, for prodding me to write more, for reminiscing with me the snippets from our eventful childhood. Talking with you all provides an instant fillip to my writing.

Thankful to my husband and son, my stalwart supporters, for enabling the time and space to write and revise, for your limitless patience with me, for loving me despite myself, for lifting my spirit on nasty days, for brainstorming possible titles and endings with me. To my in-laws for their constant love and support, for cheering me along the way.

To my writer friends, Sudha Balagopal, Myna Chang, and Jaya Wagle for reading the early drafts of this book, for your gentle critique, careful observations, and insightful suggestions. I deeply value your time, opinion, and friendship.

To Kathy Fish, Francine Witte, Kim Magowan, and Damyanti Biswas for taking the time to read the manuscript and graciously sharing your thoughts on it. I admire you as stellar writers and respect you as kind humans. Your support means more to me than I could ever express.

Forever grateful to the online writing community for standing with me and celebrating my little successes. To my FlB writing group for workshopping my stories in a collaborative, friendly environment. You inspire me to write more and better.

To the readers of my stories for upholding and uplifting me. Thanks for your time and attention to my work, for the love you bestowed upon my debut collection Morsels of Purple. Without your unflinching support, my books and all my words would have remained locked inside my head.

Indebted to *Chestnut Review* and James Rawlings for believing in my work, for making this book a reality. Immense gratitude to Maria Picone for your keen editorial eye and the clear vision, for the invaluable suggestions and edits, for your patience during the editing process. Without your help and guidance, this book would have remained an early draft. To Haley Aldrich for carefully proofreading my work. Oodles of thanks to Oormila Vijayakrishnan Prahlad for providing a face to the book, for capturing its essence in her brush strokes.

Three of these stories have appeared previously in a different form in the following publications:

"Piercings" published in *Dead Housekeeping*
"A Treacherous Fruit" in *National Flash Fiction Day Anthology*
"Ramadan" in *Delphinium*

About the Author

Sara Siddiqui Chansarkar is an Indian American writer. Born to a middle-class family in India, she later migrated to the USA with her husband and son. She currently lives in the suburbs of Ohio. She is a technologist by profession and a writer by passion. Her stories and poems have appeared in numerous publications, print and online. Her work has been selected for Best Small Fictions 2022. She won first place in *ELJ Micro Creative Non-Fiction Prize*, placed in the *Strands International Flash Fiction Festival*, and is the runner-up for the *Chestnut Review Chapbook Contest*. Her stories have been shortlisted in the *Bath Flash Fiction Awards* and *SmokeLong Micro Competition*. She is currently a Prose Editor at *Janus Literary* and a Submissions Editor at *SmokeLong Quarterly*. Her debut flash fiction collection *Morsels of Purple* was released in 2021. More at https://saraspunyfingers.com. Reach her @ PunyFingers

Made in the USA
Middletown, DE
25 July 2022